Grandpa's Bright Ideas

Written and illustrated by Bob Wilson

“Oh no! Do I have to?” said Tilly. She didn’t want to go shopping. Not with Grandpa.

"Yes, you do," said her mother. "We need to get the vacuum cleaner from the repair shop. I can't leave it to Grandpa. You know what he's like."

Tilly knew exactly what Grandpa was like. He wore his slippers in the street. He told shop assistants funny stories and then forgot what he'd come in for.

He was embarrassing.

Once, Tilly had fallen and twisted her ankle in the shopping mall. Grandpa had pushed her all the way home in a supermarket trolley.

Grandpa made you look a fool.

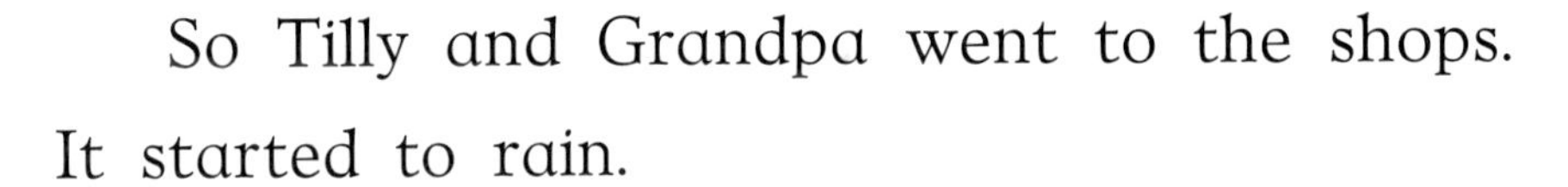

So Tilly and Grandpa went to the shops. It started to rain.

"We're going to get soaked," said Tilly.

"No we're not," said Grandpa. "I know what we need."

Nearby was a shop that sold umbrellas.

But Grandpa didn't go into the umbrella shop. Instead he went into the greengrocer's. Tilly decided to stay outside. She was glad she did.

Through the window she could see Grandpa balancing a banana on his nose.

When Grandpa came out he was carrying two cardboard boxes.

He poked eye-holes in the side of each box with his penknife. Then he gave one to Tilly.

“Put this on your head.”

“Why?” said Tilly.

“Stop you getting wet, of course,” replied Grandpa.

“But people will think I’m mad,” said Tilly.

“Who cares what other people think?” said Grandpa.

Tilly glared at Grandpa as she put the box on her head.

Tilly had to walk down the High Street wearing the cardboard box.

"Why couldn't you have bought an umbrella?"

"Umbrellas cost money," replied Grandpa.

Just then Mrs Clare came out of the hairdresser and noticed that it was raining. She didn't want to ruin her new hairstyle. She started to run.

She ran as fast as she could.

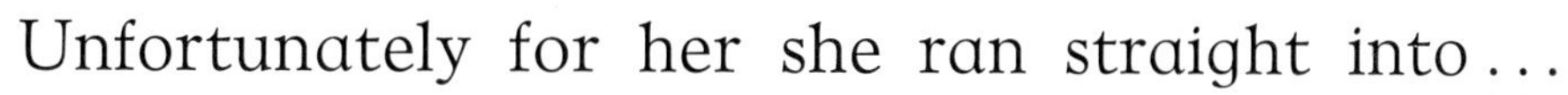

Unfortunately for her she ran straight into . . .

. . . Grandpa.

Her handbag flew through the air and went skidding down the pavement.

Grandpa took off his box and tried to help, but Mrs Clare wouldn't let him.

"Why don't you look where you're going? Fancy wearing a box on your head! What kind of an idiot are you?" she yelled.

Then she snatched up her handbag and stormed off.

"What a strange woman," said Grandpa.

A strange man was standing in a doorway. When Mrs Clare dropped her handbag, he saw the money inside.

When Mrs Clare stormed off, the stranger followed her.

Grandpa put the box back on his head.

"Tell me, Tilly, what kind of an idiot do I look like?"

"A space monster kind of an idiot," said Tilly.

"Well, fancy that!" said Grandpa.

A few minutes later, Tilly and Grandpa were in the repair shop.

Grandpa was singing into the vacuum cleaner tube. He was pretending to be a pop star. Tilly was at the back of the shop. She was pretending to be with someone else.

Suddenly from outside there came a shout: "Stop, thief!"

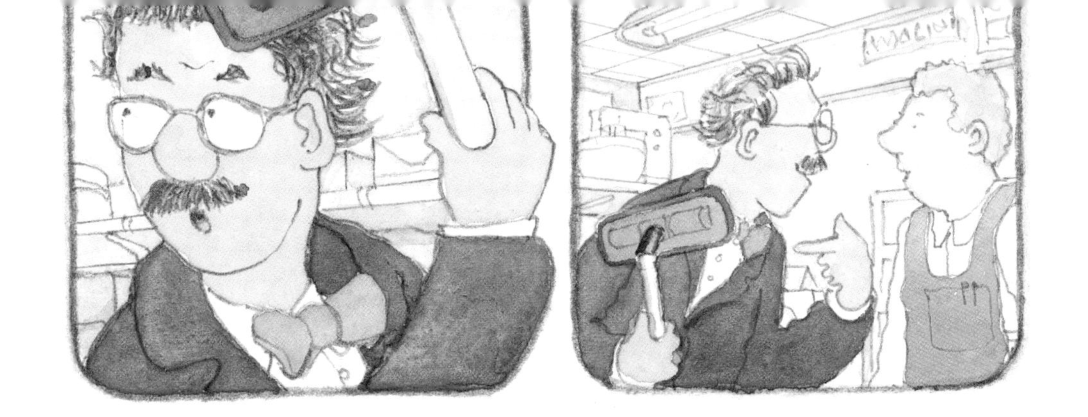

“Sounds like somebody needs my help,” said Grandpa.

He put the cardboard box back on his head, tucked the vacuum cleaner under his arm and strode out of the shop.

“Oh no,” said Tilly in despair. “What’s he up to now?” She went after him.

The handbag thief was hiding in a doorway. He peeked around the corner.

"There he is!" shouted Mrs Clare. "That's him!"

The thief's heart sank. He'd been spotted. He'd have to run for it or he'd be caught.

So he did. He ran as fast as he could.
Unfortunately for him he ran straight into...

...an alien space monster!

"STOP WHERE YOU ARE, EARTHLING!" boomed Grandpa.

"GIVE US THE BAG OR YOU WILL BE HOOVERIZED."

"AARGH!" wailed the thief.

He thrust the handbag into Tilly's hands – and ran.

Tilly was holding the bag when Mrs Clare arrived.

"Oh my dear, brave, girl!" she cried.

"It wasn't me, it was Grandpa," said Tilly.

"Why, thank you," said Mrs Clare. "I must buy you something. What would you like?"

"An umbrella would come in handy!" said Grandpa.